HAVING A SLEEPOVER

by Harold T. Rober

BUMBA BOOKS™

LERNER PUBLICATIONS ◆ MINNEAPOLIS

Note to Educators:

Throughout this book, you'll find critical thinking questions. These can be used to engage young readers in thinking critically about the topic and in using the text and photos to do so.

Lerner Publications Company
A division of Lerner Publishing Group, Inc.
241 First Avenue North
Minneapolis, MN 55401 USA

For reading levels and more information, look up this title at www.lernerbooks.com.

Library of Congress Cataloging-in-Publication Data

Names: Rober, Harold T., author.
Title: Having a sleepover / by Harold T. Rober.
Description: Minneapolis : Lerner Publications, [2017] | Series: Bumba books. Fun firsts | Includes bibliographical references and index.
Identifiers: LCCN 2016022431 (print) | LCCN 2016026273 (ebook) | ISBN 9781512425550 (lb : alk. paper) | ISBN 9781512429282 (pb : alk. paper) | ISBN 9781512427516 (eb pdf)
Subjects: LCSH: Sleepovers—Juvenile literature. | Children's parties—Juvenile literature.
Classification: LCC GV1205 .R54 2017 (print) | LCC GV1205 (ebook) | DDC 793.2/1—dc23

LC record available at https://lccn.loc.gov/2016022431

Manufactured in the United States of America
1 – VP – 12/31/16

Expand learning beyond the printed book. Download free, complementary educational resources for this book from our website, www.lernerresource.com.

Table of Contents

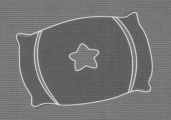

Time for a Sleepover

Sleepovers are exciting!

It is fun to have a sleepover.

Parents bring their kids to sleepovers.

Then parents pick kids up the next day.

Sleepovers last all night.

What do you need to bring to a sleepover?

Snacks are part of many sleepovers. Sometimes there is popcorn. Other times there may be pretzels.

What are some other snacks you could eat at a sleepover?

9

Kids play games at sleepovers.

They may make forts too.

Sleeping in a fort is fun!

Time to get ready for bed!

Kids put on their pajamas.

They brush their teeth.

13

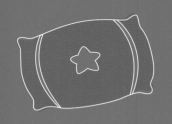

Next they get their sleeping

spots ready.

Unroll the sleeping bags!

Get out the pillows!

Soon it is time to turn off the lights.

Kids may watch movies just before lights out.

What are some other fun things to do at a sleepover?

Kids may talk even after the lights are out.

But soon it is time to sleep.

It is time for breakfast

in the morning.

Parents pick their kids up.

It was a fun sleepover!

Sleepover Supplies

sleeping bag

pillow

pajamas

floss

toothpaste

toothbrush

Picture Glossary

forts

shelters that kids build

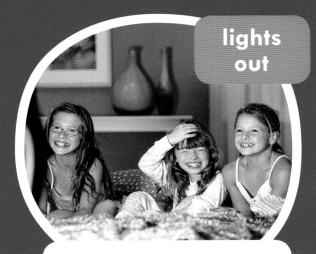

lights out

bedtime, or when lights are turned off

sleepovers

parties where one or more kids stay overnight at someone's house

unroll

to open something

Index

Read More

Heos, Bridget. *Manners at a Friend's House.* Mankato, MN: Amicus, 2016.

Lindeen, Mary. *Playing Together.* Chicago: Norwood House Press, 2016.

Rober, Harold T. *Going Camping.* Minneapolis: Lerner Publications, 2017.

Photo Credits